Lonny

the Long-Armed Puppeteer

A Real Apology

Book 2

DREW NOWLIN

AuthorHouse™
1663 Liberty Drive
Bloomington, IN 47403
www.authorhouse.com
Phone: 1 (800) 839-8640

Published by AuthorHouse 08/02/2019

ISBN: 978-1-5462-6427-9 (sc)
ISBN: 978-1-5462-6426-2 (e)

Print information available on the last page.

Any people depicted in stock imagery provided by Getty Images are models, and such images are being used for illustrative purposes only. Certain stock imagery © Getty Images.

This book is printed on acid-free paper.

Because of the dynamic nature of the Internet, any web addresses or links contained in this book may have changed since publication and may no longer be valid. The views expressed in this work are solely those of the author and do not necessarily reflect the views of the publisher, and the publisher hereby disclaims any responsibility for them.

Since we're cool we're here to say,
We love to laugh and sing all day.
Lonny dare not disobey
He'll stretch his arms to his dismay.
Telling us to stay away
But jumping rope is cool this way.
After this we'll eat sorbet,
And sit in tanning beds, hooray!
Count to ten to end this play
And win a cruise to San Jose
1... 2... 3... 4... 5...
6... 7... 8... 9... 10...Yay!

"This unfortunate rhyme was concocted by those spoiled, so called, girls that think the sun rises and sets on them. I've nicknamed this annoying group the Tiffany Trio, as they are all named Tiffany. Every Friday, to commemorate the end of the week, the Tiffany's stretch my arms for double dutch and sing this ridiculous song while jumping. I gotta give them credit for some of the rhymes, but the fact that this rhyme goes on for as long as it does is really demeaning. Luckily it does not happen any more, since a recent rumor has convinced them that playing with unpopular kids, like me, causes pimple breakouts. I wonder who could've started such a rumor.'

Lonny McMurray

Living in any town has its advantages and disadvantages. One advantage in living in a small town where every adult knows one another is that the kids can go off on their own to play and the parents never have to get into a feverish worry about where they are. Lonny and his sister, Krissy, were responsible children anyway, so their parents gave them all the freedom they needed. If the weather was nice on the weekends and they had finished all their chores, then they could go out on their own to entertain themselves. Lonny being the eldest of the two had learned long ago that whenever he and his sister went out he would have to be the one to look out for her. It is the burden of every older sibling to take some responsibility for the younger, no matter the personal cost. Lonny always called rules such as these the '*Unwritten Laws of Leverage*'. Basically it meant that these laws and tests were created by parents to help guide children towards learning responsibility and set the kids up to be blackmailed later on, should they not do well. Though parents never confessed such practices to their kids, these imaginative and strange methods of parenting seemed rather funny to Lonny. He kept telling himself such ideas were crazy, but despite the fact he was aware of this and knew most of the '*Unwritten Laws of Leverage*', he didn't care. Lonny really didn't mind taking his sister for a Saturday excursion when she asked. It gave him a warm and proud feeling.

On this particular Saturday the McMurray kids found themselves in a nice area, just under the tree line, that overlooked the new construction site a short ways from the main road. The sun shone bright through the leaves and a faint wind rustled the treetops carrying the sweet smell of summer vacation that was right around the corner. It had rained a few days ago and the ground was still a little damp in some areas, but overall today was a great day to get out. A few yards away the construction site was simply fenced off and cleared away for next month's big fast food restaurant build. No one was working that weekend and there was no noise or giant equipment in the area to indicate danger, so Lonny and Krissy decided this dry patch of ground was as good a place as any to sit and enjoy the day. Lonny was reading a book about birds of prey, while Krissy had a selection of her dolls, along with a couple of zombie puppets Lonny had made for her. She was playing in her own little world, making different voices for the dolls, and Lonny had all but tuned out the noise she was making. After a little while, Lonny dropped his book and gazed and the familiar stretch of land that was not so familiar anymore.

This spot had long been one of Lonny's favorite places to go when it was still just trees and shrubs. He'd often escape here so he wouldn't have to deal with the teasing of the other kids, like Alex Brimley, or the stuck up rantings of the Tiffany Trio. There used to be a very tall Oak tree that stood in the middle of that baron field that had a strange series of knots that grew out of one side. Somehow the collection of knots resembled a smiling face, and Lonny was always made happier when he saw that tree smiling at him without reason or judgment.

However, now it was gone and a faint sense of loss entered his heart.

Lonny's memories were interrupted by some local boys that had jumped the safety fence and were roughhousing in the desolate patch of Earth. They were carrying on and playing tag in a mud hole that hadn't dried yet. Lonny didn't recognize them, because they were a few years older, but he was content enough to go back to his book.

'Hey,' cried Krissy with a zombie puppet on her arm. 'Why are you reading a book instead of playing?'

'I'm just inspired by nature right now and I'm thinking of making a bird puppet,' Lonny stated with his eyes still glued to the pages.

'Oh by the way,' Krissy remembered. 'Thank you for making me these zombies. It's so hard to find quality zombie puppets. Most of the zombie stuff is action figures.'

'Your welcome,' Lonny chuckled. 'What are big brothers for?'

'I especially like the one with the eye hanging out of his socket,' Krissy confessed. 'He's always the most hungry for flesh, aren't you cutie,' she said kissing the puppet on the mouth.

Lonny looked at her as she did so. He couldn't help but feel just a tad bit disgusted, but then he slowly poked his head up and looked back to the empty plot. 'Do you remember an old tree with a kinda face on it?'

'Kinda,' Krissy said as the zombie puppet wrapped its mouth around one of her doll's heads. 'It had a creepy face on it. I'm glad it's gone.'

'Creepy?' Lonny exclaimed turning towards her again. 'You are calling something creepy?'

'Yeah,' Krissy said smiling at him. Then before she could finish her statement, a ball of mud and grime hit her in the back of the head. It was like time had slowed to a crawl as Lonny saw the damp projectile engulf his sister's head. Lonny dropped his book immediately and rushed over to her. She was hunched over, trying desperately not to cry, but Lonny knew his sister and could tell the impact hurt. He cleared off the mud and saw that she wasn't bleeding, but she was still rattled. The faint sound of laughing grew louder as the group of boys rushed to the fence. Krissy didn't turn around to face them but held on tight to Lonny's arm as he looked at the hoodlums.

'Hey,' Lonny shouted. 'Why don't you be more careful? You could've really hurt her.'

'Is she ok?' One of the boys inquired, still with a smirk on his face.

Lonny looked at her and she turned her head towards him and gave a small nod. Her eyes were still watered over and Lonny looked back. 'She'd be doing better if you would at least apologize for what you did,' Lonny commented as he cast his eyes back at Krissy, who nodded again.

'She's Ok though right?' The boy repeated.

'Well she's not bleeding,' Lonny sneered, still expecting that apology.

'Cool,' the boy casually said and then ran off, followed by the others.

Lonny sat there astonished. His chest felt as if it was made of iron, from the weight of this realization. He couldn't talk or move for what seemed like hours. How could someone be so blatantly inconsiderate? Did no one but him care about what just happened?

'That didn't sound like an apology to me,' Krissy finally mumbled. Lonny snapped back to reality.

'It didn't sound like one to me either,' Lonny said softly. 'You Ok?'

'Yeah,' Krissy said while she got to her feet and started picking up her toys. 'But they got mud on my favorite puppet. I feel all bisfoozzled now.'

'I'll clean it off and make him look just like new,' Lonny promised. 'But first I'll take you home.' Lonny felt a tinge of utter rage in the depths of his stomach. He turned Krissy to face him and looked her right in the eyes. 'I promise you sis, that boy will apologize for what he did, Ok?'

Krissy looked at him, wiped the tears from her eyes, and smiled. 'That would be good,' she said. And the two of them went home together.

******

Lonny spent the entire week trying to devise a plan on how to get his sister that apology, but to achieve this goal there were a few things to consider. Firstly, Lonny didn't want to get parents involved in any way, so he couldn't do anything too drastic that would result in him getting in trouble. Secondly, the target was a bit older than him and any revenge could possibly lead to some brutal consequences due to the lack of parental involvement. And finally, the apology had to be sincere. Anything less would not satisfy him or Krissy.

Lonny learned the target's name was Vince and that his home was only a few blocks away. Vince was a middle

school student and Lonny knew several of Vince's classmates, but despite everything he could not come up with a great idea to achieve his victory. No matter how angry or frustrated a situation was, Lonny knew that he was not a truly spiteful person. Therefore, Lonny knew that he was in a difficult position.

It was Friday. Lonny sat on the front porch, of that next to last house on Sunset Avenue, leaning his head onto his hands. His eyes gazed at the horizon, still fixated on the task at hand, but morally torn between what would happen with each passing idea. Off in the distance, the dull hum of the last school bus was fading down the road. Suddenly Lonny jumped at the sould of a door slaming. It was his neighbor, Mr. Falco, coming outside to enjoy a bit of fresh air. He did this the same couple times every day, but being a former soldier it didn't seem so uncommon. Mr. Falco was in a wheelchair as a result of the Vietnam War, but he refused to let a wheelchair define him. He rolled himself to the edge of his front ramp to sit in the sunshine and sip on a glass of lemonade, conveniently cushioned in his wheelchair's cup holder. He was wearing a very drab, grey shirt and his camouflage fatigue pants. For an elderly man he was quite energetic and full of life. He really didn't have a lot of wrinkles for an old guy and he had a firm, square jaw line, silver trimmed hair, and a muscular physique. Mr. Falco was still an intimidating citizen when he wanted to be, yet the majority of the time he was incredibly insightful and kind. Lonny had developed a deep respect for Mr. Falco's spirit and wisdom over the years.

'Hey rubber band man,' Mr. Falco exclaimed upon noticing his little friend. 'How bout a five yard high five?' Lonny chuckled, forgetting his troubles for a moment and extended his right arm towards Mr. Falco and gave him a high five. 'Come on over and check out my new wheel reflectors, Mr. Stretchington!' Lonny did not mind Mr. Falco coming up with strange names for him, because he knew

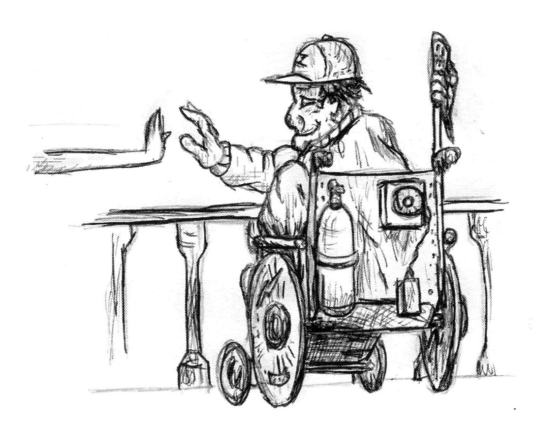

it was out of friendship and not fear. In fact, Mr. Falco had told Lonny a while back that he enjoyed the company of children. It reminded him of simpler times and of days long past when he could run and be enthralled with youthful imagination. Mr. Falco had even encouraged Lonny to come up with some outlandish names for him since it was all in good fun. He was a really funny man.

'Alright hot wheels,' Lonny casually responded with a smile creeping across his face, since Mr. Falco's outrageous wheelchair gadgets always intrigued him. Lonny shrunk his arm to normal size, stood up and started across the yard to talk with his friend. 'How are you doing today?' He asked as he slowly strode across the green grass.

'Well I'm still stuck in this blasted chair, but other than that I feel pretty darn good,' Falco said as he lifted a glass of lemonade to his lips, taking a sip. 'Ah it's a beautiful day,' he continued. 'It's much too beautiful a day to be moping around on your front porch. Why not experience what life has to offer and get out there and do something?' Lonny gave no reply. Mr. Falco took a long look at him when Lonny reached the bottom the ramp then leaned back in his chair and lowered his booming voice. 'I've seen that face many a time before and in my experience it can mean one of three things. You either had a family quarrel, you've discovered girls, or you're just stuck. So which is it my flexible friend?'

Mr. Falco had a keen ability of being observant and very blunt, but he knew because he was old and handicapped he could act any way he wanted and no one would hold it against him. 'Well,' Lonny hesitated with a somewhat embarrassed look on his face. 'Someone hurt my sister's feelings and didn't say they were sorry. Now I'm trying to figure out how to get him to apologize to her and mean it.'

'I see,' Mr. Falco acknowledged. 'So basically you're torn about what to do. It'd be so easy to dangle him off a building with them long arms of yours huh? But what would that do except make things even worse, right?' He chuckled under his breathe and placed his lemonade back in its holder.

'Something like that Mr. Falco,' Lonny admitted.

'Well son, welcome to the human condition,' Mr. Falco continued. 'And just for this conversation I want you to call me Mitch. Come on and sit down here for a spell.' Lonny was a little taken back for a moment, for he never knew what Mr. Falco's first name was. 'You're a bright boy, but no matter how smart anyone is, sooner or later everyone is tempted to resort to simple revenge to solve certain problems. It's the same old story; if something or someone precious to you is put in danger, you feel it's your duty to resolve the problem quickly and decisively.'

'Yeah,' Lonny said with a hint of relief in his voice as he sat beside his friend.

'Well stretch, I hate to tell you this, but no matter what you come up with it isn't gonna work,' Mitch confided in a tone Lonny had never heard before. 'This sorta situation always ends badly. I can't tell you how many friends I lost over something so trivial and so stupid as meaningless fighting.' Mr. Falco paused for a moment and a veil of sadness crossed his face. He looked to Lonny then quickly regained his composure. 'But the answer is quite simple. The strategy you need to consider is one of karma.'

'Karma?' Lonny thought for a moment. 'Isn't that the idea that if you do something good, good things will come to you?'

'Precisely, my elastic comrade, and the opposite is true as well' Mitch boasted. 'Basically it refers to cause and effect. This strategy is more along the lines of mind games and psychology. You don't need to do anything drastic, just give him a few pushes in the right direction and the rest will take care of itself.'

A wave of inspiration fell upon Lonny and he was finally able to come up with a terribly simple, yet effective plan. Lonny sprung to his feet in excitement.

'Thank you Mr.....' Lonny began.

'Ahh ....' Mr. Falco interrupted.

'Oh right! Thank you for your advice, Mitch. I know it will come in handy,' Lonny said.

'No problem,' Mitch said. 'If you ever need any

more words of wisdom, I'll always be within arms reach. Now go on and get that apology.' Lonny hurried back across the yard to his house. 'Oh and don't forget to come over next Saturday,' Mr. Falco

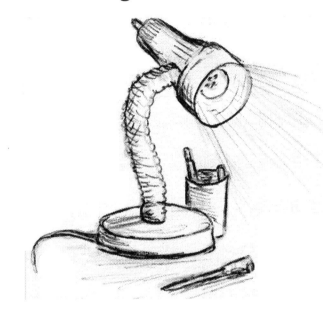

yelled. 'The new headlights and music speakers for my wheelchair should arrive, so we can go cruising for eligible ladies.'

******

After another day of preparation and a few phone calls, it was late in the afternoon on Sunday and Lonny decided to confront Vince at his own home. The day was overcast and everyone knew a storm would hit them by late evening. Lonny noticed that Vince lived in a rather lavish two-story home. The windows were large and there were trees surrounding the sides and back of the home. The lawn was well trimmed and a peculiar lawn gnome figure holding a lantern cast a strange smirk at Lonny as he walked to the front door. The home was painted a really bizarre shade of blue with white trim and molding. Not a bad place.

Lonny rang the doorbell and waited. After a few moments Vince came to the door.

'Yeah,' he muffled as he was finishing off a sandwich.

'Hi Vince,' Lonny said, remembering not to say his name.

'Do we know eachother?' Vince asked with a bit of whimsical curiosity.

'Not really, but we did speak a week or so ago when you hit my sister with a mud ball,' Lonny replied.

'Oh yeah,' Vince remembered. 'So what do you want?'

'My sister is still waiting for her apology,' Lonny sternly stated, never taking his eyes away from Vince's.

'It's over, so why do you need one?' Vince said jokingly.

'Well it's just common courtesy and I'm afraid I must insist,' Lonny calmly suggested.

'And what if I don't?' Vince inquired. 'What are you gonna do, tell on me?'

'No I'm afraid I'll have to put a hex on you,' Lonny said, as he pulled out a mask that he had been holding behind his back. He put the mask on his face. The mask was nearly featureless except for very large, dark eyes. There was no mouth, nose, or really any cheeks of any sort on the mask. It was painted to look like rolling ocean waves, but instead of blues and whites the waves were painted with reds and oranges. Lonny stared at Vince and reiterated, 'I'm asking you to apologize or else bad luck will follow you until you do. All you need to do is say you are sorry and it will be lifted.'

'Forget it,' Vince said. 'I make great grades, have several beautiful girls calling me, and I'm an extremely popular football player. And you are going to hex me? Do your worst.' And Vince slammed the door in Lonny's face and all Lonny could hear was laughing fading upstairs. Lonny took a few steps back and looked to the second floor. He saw the lights flicker on in one of the rooms and Vince appeared. While still wearing the mask, Lonny simply turned and walked away. He thought to himself that his tasks would have to be consistent in order for it to work and tomorrow was Monday, so let it begin.

Monday was here at last. Lonny convinced Krissy that they ride their bicycles to school this week so they could make a pit stop every morning and not be late for class. This Monday morning was foggy, but there was no rain so they rode for Vince's house just in time to see Vince's bus heading for the middle school. Now that no one was home, Lonny slipped a folded piece of paper into Vince's mailbox and into the crevice of the front door. The folded note merely had the word 'apology' written on it. Lonny got back on his bike and smiled at his little sister. He had not told Krissy what his plan was, but had assured her that by the end of the week she would most likely have her apology. For now though their work was done and they both rode for school.

After school was over Lonny rode back to his house to drop off Krissy, but then headed off to Vince's home once more. Middle school students get out a bit later than elementary school kids and that fact was in Lonny's favor. Lonny pulled around the corner to the house and saw that the bus was just a stop away from its drop off. Lonny ducked out of site and pulled out the red mask he'd shown Vince before. He put it on and waited for a moment. The bus pulled to a screeching stop and Vince hopped off first and ran for his front door. As Vince fumbled through some keys, he noticed the folded message on the door and opened it. Just as he did so, Lonny came riding by with the mask on and simply stared at Vince.

Vince stood on his front door stoop and just chuckled and crumpled the paper in his hand. Lonny turned down the next road and went home with a sense of accomplishment. The first day was over.

A bright and clear Tuesday morning dawned and it was day two of the plan. Lonny did the same thing he'd done before, but instead of one note he dropped two in the mailbox and two in the door. After another day of higher learning, Lonny stopped off at Vince's house again waiting for him. This time Lonny brought Krissy along and gave her a mask exactly like his. When Vince got to his front door and looked at the two notes, he turned to behold two masked figures riding past him with dark, menacing stares. Today Vince seemed less amused and hurried into his home with haste and locked the door. Lonny and Krissy rounded the corner and when they were out of sight took off their masks.

'Are we doing something bad to him?' Krissy asked with a sour look across her face.

Lonny did not want his sister to regret what they were doing. 'No we are not doing anything wrong. Trust me,' Lonny stated. 'He needs to be taught a lesson and we are doing nothing to hurt him. I just want to make him see that his attitude hurts people. If he just apologizes it would stop, but by the end of the week whether he's apologized or not it will all be over. OK?'

Krissy gave her brother a smile and took a sigh of relief as they wheeled off towards home with him following close behind. Lonny's conscience was wrestling with him as well, but be didn't tell that to his little sister. Lonny knew this was the only way to teach Vince that he must take responsibility for his own actions. Suddenly Lonny realized that he was writing his own page for the book of *'Unwritten Laws of Leverage'*. Lonny peddled his bike and a smile of amazement crossed his face.

'This is crazy,' Lonny shouted. He laughed at himself all the way home. He was in the middle of a plan that was so brilliant and so stupid at the same time. 'I'm not even a parent yet and look what I'm doing,' Lonny said to himself and that revelation gave him new resolve to finish what he started.

And a windy Wednesday morning began and the weather report said there would be rain in the afternoon. The sky was gray and all remnants of yesterday's great weather were veiled by the clouds. Once again the two siblings rode to the house and Lonny dropped off three notes in the mailbox and in the door, but there was one more thing to do. He took one of the red masks and stretched his arms up the tree outside Vince's bedroom window. Lonny pulled himself to a sturdy branch and tied his mask into the tree limbs, so that it faced the bedroom widow. Lonny carefully came down and he led his sister to school. Later that day Vince came home and immediately tore up the notes in the door and mailbox apart. The rain was beginning to fall and Vince saw no trace of anyone wearing a mask. He entered his house cautiously and began to feel a bit more relaxed as he walked upstairs and opened his bedroom door. Vince peered out his window to make sure that no one was riding by when he spied the mask hanging in the tree. Lonny was standing a good distance away and watching Vince under and umbrella without any mask on. Lonny saw that Vince was unnerved and decided that tomorrow was the last time.

Thursday brought a terrible downpour of rain. Mr. McMurray took both his kids to school that morning, so they wouldn't get damp. When the final bell of the day rang, Lonny and Krissy's mom picked them up and brought them back home. The rain had stopped by that time and Lonny had one more thing to do. He took off on his bike and went to Vince's house. He put his bike around the back corner of the house and walked to the front door. He put a smaller version of the mask on the strange lawn gnome in the yard then went to the tree where his other mask was still hanging. Lonny stretched his arms to the branch and raised himself into the foliage. Lonny could hear the bus in the distance drawing ever closer. This was it. If Vince was finally ready to apologize then Lonny could keep his promise to his sister and restore her dignity. The bus's wheels hissed as the bus came to a stop and the rusty doors squeaked open and closed. Lonny saw Vince from his treetop perch. Vince didn't look good at all and, upon seeing the mask Lonny had left on the gnome, Vince stopped and stood staring at it.

'Ok, ok,' Vince said aloud. 'I'm tired of this.' Lonny sat in the tree in case Vince was so mad he might try to take his anger out on him.

'Are you ready to say you are sorry to my sister?' Lonny asked from high above.

Vince caught sight of Lonny and walked to the tree. 'Why did you do this?' Vince asked.

'I'm sorry Vince,' Lonny pleaded. 'I didn't want to do it, but you really hurt my sister's feelings that day. All I wanted was for you to sincerely admit you felt bad for doing that and grow up a bit. I gave you every opportunity to stop it, but you didn't do it. This can stop right now if you give Krissy that apology.' Lonny could tell that Vince was not full of rage or malice by the way he stood there.

'We lost our football game, my grades are slipping, and I'm not as popular anymore,' Vince confessed. 'Did you do all that?'

'No,' Lonny admitted. 'All I'm guilty of is a few scraps of paper and a couple masks. Everything else was just coincidence. Maybe it was fate telling you to do something right, I don't know. I don't have any magical powers.. .' Lonny had to stop and think for a minute. 'Well... no powers that could cause anything like THAT to happen, but I hope you can appreciate that I did what I did because a family member was hurting and I wanted to make it right.'

'I can understand and appreciate that,' Vince sighed.

'Good,' Lonny said as he detached the mask from the tree limb. He peered down at Vince. 'One way or another, this is over today. This is the last time I will ask for a genuine apology. Whether you give it to Krissy or not, the notes, masks, and make-believe hexes will end. What do you say?'

Vince smiled and nodded his head. 'Yeah, you're right,' Vince admitted. 'I'll give that apology to your sister.'

'Thank you,' Lonny said as he grabbed the tree limb and slowly lowered himself onto the ground. Vince was struck by surprise.

'I had no idea you

were the stretchy kid that some of my friends talk about,' Vince exclaimed.

'Pretty cool, huh?' Lonny confessed. 'Sometimes it does have its advantages. So my house is right around the corner.'

Lonny removed the mask from the gnome and put both masks in his bag. The two boys made their way back to the McMurray home as the clouds began to part in the sky and the sun illuminated what seemed like the entire world.

******

'I am deeply sorry for what I did and I am glad you are alright,' Vince said as he stood in the doorway of Lonny's house with Krissy right there in front of him. He'd explained all that had happened to him over the past couple of days and Krissy seemed very sorry for the whole ordeal. Krissy looked up at the tall boy and took his hand with both of hers.

'I appreciate and accept your apology,' Krissy said with a smile on her face. She shook his hand and let it go. 'And you are always welcome to come by and watch zombie movies with me if you want.'

'Ok,' Vince said with a curious hesitation in his response.

Krissy walked back into her home and Lonny stepped forward and handed him a folded up piece of paper.

'Don't worry,' Lonny said. 'It's just an open invitation to my next puppet show. I'm working on a talking tree puppet that gives some good advice to a bird that perches in its branches. I hope it will be good, but I'm still not sure how the script will turn out.'

'Sounds great,' Vince said accepting the gift. 'Oh just not on a football night, Ok?'

'Ok!' Lonny stated and he closed the door as Vince left for home. Lonny took a big breath of accomplishment and relief that this ordeal was really over. He leaned his head against the door and shut his eyes to enjoy the moment. When he regained himself he turned only to be confronted by Krissy. She had a peculiar look on her face and her eyes were squinting as she looked at him. 'Is something wrong?'

'I appreciate that you kept your promise,' she said.

'Thanks,' Lonny stated.

'But did you have anything to do with that other stuff he was talking about?' Krissy inquired.

'I had nothing to do with the football game or the grades,' Lonny confessed. Krissy still looked at him with squinty eyes like she didn't completely believe him. 'Seriously, that's it.'

'Really?' Krissy insisted.

'Ok,' Lonny regretfully admitted. 'I called up some popular girls in his school and asked them to act interested in him on Monday, but to go back to normal after that.' Krissy had this annoying way of ferreting out the truth from her brother.

'So they didn't break up with him because of you?' Krissy asked. She wanted to make sure that her brother didn't sink to a new low.

'No,' Lonny quickly replied. 'They told me that the reason they don't really like him is because he picks his nose.'

'Oh,' Krissy exclaimed. 'Well that's understandable. It's a nasty habit.' The investigative expression left her face as she turned and walked to her bedroom. 'Oh yeah,' Krissy remembered. 'If you have some free time while building that puppet show, with the tree in it you were talking about, could we go out again on Saturday?'

'Yeah, no problem,' Lonny said. 'And remind me to stop by Mr. Falco's place. He's got some new stuff for his wheelchair that he wanted me to see.'

'Yes I love my sister so sue me. Now for you kids around my age thinking of doing what I did to Vince to someone you know, please don't. A lot of stuff could have happened differently and the best idea is always to talk to your Mom and Dad. But even if a situation like this doesn't happen, ask them about the '*Unwritten Laws of Leverage*'. They may say they don't know what you are talking about, but tell them to read this book and they'll remember quickly. Even then they may not admit to it, but that is a parent's right anyway, so be understanding. Who knows, you might realize your doing it when you have kids. Come back and share another adventure with me and my stretchy arms again. Oh, before I forget, Mr. Falco is a great friend of mine. If you know of any people that have served for our country show them respect. Especially if they are much, much, much, much, much, older than you are ….. I'm talking ancient here.'

Lonny McMurray

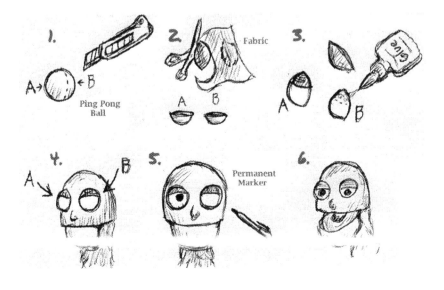

Printed in the United States
By Bookmasters